XERKAN
THE SHAPE STEALER

WITHDRAWN

BY ADAM BLADE

ORCHARD

With special thanks to Conrad Mason

www.beastquest.co.uk

ORCHARD BOOKS

First published in Great Britain in 2019 by The Watts Publishing Group

1 3 5 7 9 10 8 6 4 2

Text © 2019 Beast Quest Limited.
Cover and inside illustrations by Steve Sims
© Beast Quest Limited 2019

Beast Quest is a registered trademark of Beast Quest Limited
Series created by Beast Quest Limited, London

A CIP catalogue record for this book is available from the British Library.

ISBN 978 1 40834 349 4

Printed in Great Britain

The paper and board used in this book are made from wood from responsible sources

Orchard Books
An imprint of Hachette Children's Group
Part of The Watts Publishing Group Limited
Carmelite House, 50 Victoria Embankment, London EC4Y 0DZ

An Hachette UK Company
www.hachette.co.uk
www.hachettechildrens.co.uk

Welcome to the world of Beast Quest!

Tom was once an ordinary village boy, until he travelled to the City, met King Hugo and discovered his destiny. Now he is the Master of the Beasts, sworn to defend Avantia and its people against Evil. Tom draws on the might of the magical Golden Armour, and is protected by powerful tokens granted to him by the Good Beasts of Avantia. Tom and his loyal companion Elenna are always ready to visit new lands and tackle the enemies of the realm.

While there's blood in his veins, Tom will never give up the Quest…

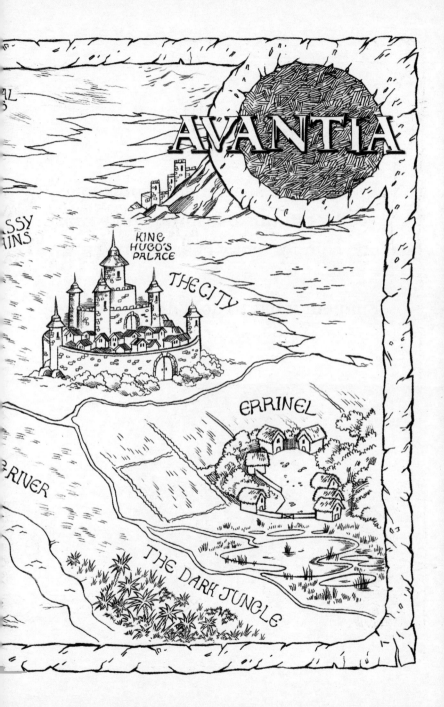

There are special gold coins to collect in this book. You will earn one coin for every chapter you read.

Find out what to do with your coins at the end of the book.

CONTENTS

It's been many years since I crossed the borders of Avantia. I can't say I've missed the place much. Last time I was here, my plan to conquer the kingdom was foiled by a mere boy, though he calls himself their Master of the Beasts.

Now I serve a new and cruel master. Though he looks like a man, he has the cold heart of a monster. We have travelled day and night from the Wildlands north of Avantia's frozen wastes, and at last the walls of the City loom into view.

I have heard the boy Tom is still alive. I wonder what he will think when he sees me again. And I wonder if he will understand the terrible danger that is about to be unleashed.

One thing is certain – the kingdom and its people are going to suffer a terrible fate.

Yours,

Kapra the Witch

PETRA'S SPELL

Tom shivered as an icy wind whipped through the valley.

If only I still had the magic of my shield, he thought. *I could use Nanook's bell to protect us from the cold...* But the new King of Avantia had taken that from him, along with all his other powers.

"I can barely feel my fingers!"

grumbled Elenna, rubbing her hands together. "Can't we go now?"

A short distance away, the witch Petra was crouching down in the ruins of her little shack, sifting bits and pieces from the rubble. She turned to glare at Elenna.

"Oh, how terrible for you," she sneered. "You might catch a chill! Meanwhile, a three-headed dragon Beast has just torn apart everything I've ever owned."

"Thanks for reminding us," said Elenna. "Again."

For once, Tom actually felt sorry for the young witch. So far Petra had salvaged half a spell book and a few little bags of potion ingredients.

Everything else had been trampled by Torka, the flying reptile Tom had just defeated.

"Just remember, her mother got us into this mess in the first place," muttered Elenna, as Petra kept on hunting through the ruins. "It was Kapra who brought that imposter to Avantia. The one pretending to be Angelo, who threw out the real King Hugo. She's obviously trying to destroy the kingdom!"

"My mother does hate Avantia," said Petra, without turning round.

"Which is why we have to get back to the City," said Elenna. "And fast!"

Tom nodded. He could still remember the horrifying things

he had seen through the magical
Sightmist. How the fake King Angelo
was tormenting the citizens with new
taxes and bullying them with his
thuggish soldiers...

"We'd better get going," he said,
shuffling his feet to keep warm.
"Whoever that imposter is, he has to
be stopped."

Petra cast him a sly smile. "Aren't
there *four* Beasts of the Wildlands?"
she asked. "You've only defeated
three. Is the great Master of the
Beasts going to just give up?"

Tom shook his head. "The fourth
Beast can wait. We've got a kingdom
to save."

Petra snorted. "Suit yourself." She

stood and slung a bag of possessions over her shoulder. "It's only a day's journey to the Icy Plains. Then about two days' ride to the City…if you can find a horse, that is."

We have to get there quicker than that…

Tom hesitated. "Can you help us?" he asked.

Petra's grin grew wider. "I must be dreaming. The mighty Tom needs help?"

Elenna rolled her eyes. "Just get on with it."

"Very well." Petra put down her bag. "My mother once taught me to make a powerful transportation potion. I've dug out all the ingredients. But if you really want my help...I'm going to need something in return."

Tom felt his cheeks getting hot. *I just hope she doesn't ask me for a kiss again!*

But instead Petra turned to

Elenna. "You have to say sorry."

"What for?" exploded Elenna.

Petra scowled. "For being mean to me all the time."

Elenna clenched her fists, but Tom laid a hand on her arm. "It's worth it," he whispered. "We need her help."

Elenna opened her mouth, then closed it again. She managed a phoney smile. "Sorry then, I suppose."

Petra clapped her hands together. "That wasn't so hard, was it? Now, get a fire going. I'll prepare the cauldron..."

As the witch turned to get started, Elenna rolled her eyes.

A short while later, Tom watched as Petra dropped one foul ingredient after another into her cauldron. First a handful of rotten old mushrooms; then a scatter of sparrows' tongues; last was a scrap of animal skin. Soon she had a thick, green liquid bubbling over the fire Tom and Elenna had made.

"It smells like a rancid bog," said Elenna, wrinkling her nose. "Are you trying to poison us?"

"Charming," sniffed Petra. "Maybe you should mix up your own magical potion of transportation."

"We trust you," said Tom, quickly. He wasn't sure he really did. *But right now she's our only hope...*

"I'll just give it one last stir," said Petra, twisting a wooden spoon in the liquid. "There! Now, we must all face south."

"Why?" asked Elenna.

Petra giggled. "What a stupid question. Because that's the way we're going, obviously."

Petra spooned her potion into three little wooden cups and passed them round. Then she stood side by side with Tom and Elenna, facing south. "Drink it all," said the witch. "Don't leave a drop!"

Tom sniffed dubiously at the thick, dark green liquid. *It really does smell like bog water!* He pinched his nose. Then they all drank the potion together.

"Urgh," gasped Elenna, throwing the cup away. "This had better work."

"My spells always work," snapped Petra. "Any...moment..."

Tom's head swam. He felt dizzy.

"...now!" finished Petra.

And suddenly Tom was rushing towards the horizon. The ground raced beneath him, even though he wasn't moving his legs. He flung out his arms, wheeling them for balance. To his right he saw Elenna doing the same. The mountains were sliding past her.

"Whoa!" she breathed.

Tom gasped. *It's working! We're going faster than a galloping horse. Faster than a soaring dragon.*

"Wheeeee!" cried Petra. Tom turned to see her on his left, speeding along with them. "Told you it would work, didn't I?"

Tom grinned as the wind buffeted his face.

The ground beneath their feet changed from rocks to icy dunes. The ice gave way to scrubby grasses and hard soil, then long grasses. The air was getting warmer.

We're flying over the Central Plains, Tom realised, in amazement.

A village flashed by in a heartbeat. They skimmed above a river. They darted through a forest, and the leaves brushed against Tom's face.

"Look!" called Elenna.

Tom saw a grey ridge on the horizon. *No, wait...* He could see flags flying from towers now, and sunshine glinting from soldiers' armour. *It's the wall of the City!* They rushed towards it, the heavy grey stones looming closer and closer.

"We're going too fast!" cried Elenna.

Tom's heart was pounding. "How do we stop?" he shouted.

"Oh, didn't I mention?" said Petra, smiling wickedly. "Like this." The witch clicked her fingers. At once she stopped dead, while Tom and Elenna went rushing on…

Click!

As Tom snapped his fingers, his stomach lurched. He went tumbling head over heels. *Thump!* He landed flat on his back, the world spinning around him. Elenna groaned, lying in a heap at his side.

Carefully, Tom pushed himself upright.

"Oi! You!"

Tom blinked. They had landed right in front of the wooden drawbridge. Four soldiers were running across it, their armour clanking, each carrying a spear and shield.

"We're Avantians," Tom said quickly. "No need to—"

"It's him!" shouted one of the soldiers. They surrounded Tom and Elenna, and crouched down behind their shields. "It's the traitor! On your feet, both of you." He pointed behind Tom, to Petra. "And grab that greasy-looking one too!"

Petra was rummaging in her bag of belongings. *She must be searching for some magical item that could help us...*

Petra drew out a little leather pouch. She winked at Tom, then threw it to the ground. *Whumph!* A puff of pink smoke rose up from the pouch. When it cleared, the witch was nowhere to be seen.

"Oh, what a surprise!" muttered Elenna.

Tom couldn't stick up for Petra this time. *She's abandoned us...*

SWIFT GARETH

The soldiers stripped them of their weapons and marched them over the drawbridge.

Funny, thought Tom, peering at the soldier holding his sword and shield. *I'm sure I recognise him...*

Then he realised. The soldier was Swift Gareth, a famous pickpocket Captain Harkman had arrested and

put in the dungeon. *What's he doing,
wearing the tunic of Avantia?*

"These aren't real soldiers," Tom
whispered to Elenna as they went
through the gateway.

"You're right," Elenna replied. "I'm
sure the one who arrested us was
barred from the City for fighting

in taverns." Tom saw that he had a
tattoo of a skull on his neck.

Tom frowned. *The imposter king
must be recruiting dangerous
criminals for his own private army!*

"Stand back!" roared Gareth,
sweeping his spear from side to side
as they strode into the city. Beggars

scuttled out of the road.

Tom could hardly believe this was the same place that he knew and loved. The streets were almost empty, and the air was thick with the smell of sweat, dirt and dung. Frightened faces peered from doorways and windows, but disappeared as soon as he looked at them.

Everyone must be terrified of the new king's soldiers.

He shivered as he caught sight of metal cages dangling from the highest rooftops, the ropes creaking as they swayed in the breeze. Skeletal prisoners crouched inside, every one filthy and underfed.

When they reached the courtyard

of the palace, Tom gasped in shock.
A chopping block still stood on
a wooden platform in the centre.
That's where the fake King Angelo
almost took my head off! But now
there were several nooses too,
dangling from a scaffold above.

"What's happened here?" breathed
Elenna, her eyes wide.

"Pretty sight, isn't it?" smirked the
soldier with the skull tattoo. "King
Angelo loves a good execution. Often
does it himself, in fact." The soldier
pointed with his spear, and Tom
saw a gleaming silver axe leaning
against the chopping block. *It's like*
something out of a nightmare!

The soldiers jostled them through

a wooden side gate, along a corridor
and down stone steps into darkness,
lit only by a few flickering torches.
Tom knew the way well.

They're taking us to the dungeon.

Sure enough, the soldiers led Tom
and Elenna past a row of barred cells
crammed with prisoners. The one at
the end was dark and empty, and Tom
and Elenna were shoved into it.

"Hope it's to your liking," sneered
Swift Gareth. He turned a key in a
lock. Then the soldiers strode off,
laughing, taking Tom and Elenna's
weapons with them.

What now? wondered Tom. He tried
to force the door of the prison cell,
but it wouldn't budge. *If only I had*

the magical strength of my golden breastplate...

"Tom!" gasped Elenna suddenly.

Spinning round, Tom saw that the cell wasn't empty after all. A bundle of rags in the corner was shifting and uncurling. Then a figure rose up, casting off the rags to reveal a filthy blue robe beneath. It was a young man, and Tom had never been so glad to see his face.

"Daltec!" he cried.

The wizard blinked and peered through the darkness. Tom saw that his wrists were tied with thick rope. "Tom? Elenna!" But his smile faded at once. "So Angelo has captured you too."

"I'm afraid so," said Tom, grimly.

"Petra brought us here with her magic."

"Then disappeared at the first sign of trouble," added Elenna.

"But what's been happening here in the City?" asked Tom. "Everything is so different."

"So much worse, you mean," said Daltec. "Yes, our new king is a tyrant. He released the very worst prisoners in Avantia and turned them into his personal army. Meanwhile the people are starving, and Angelo's new laws are cruel. Even stealing an apple is punished with death."

"What a monster," muttered Elenna.

"I sent a messenger bird to Aduro and King Hugo in Tangala, before I was arrested," said Daltec. "I just hope it reaches them in time."

"Don't worry," Tom said. "We'll find a way out of here. We'll defeat

Angelo ourselves."

Daltec smiled and shook his head. "Even you can't tackle the false king, Tom. You have no powers. And Angelo has spies everywhere. No one dares lift a finger against him."

Tom heard footsteps outside. Then Captain Harkman appeared at the cell door, his face deeply lined. Tom's heart leaped to see another old friend.

"Master of the Beasts," said Harkman, shaking his head. "Can you forgive me? The soldiers don't listen to me any more!"

"It's not your fault," said Elenna.

"I'm just glad you're not in the dungeon too," said Tom.

Harkman scowled. "He made me

swear allegiance to him. I should have refused, but he would have killed me. How can the brother of King Hugo be so cruel?"

"He's not Hugo's brother!" said Elenna. "He's an imposter."

"We found proof," Tom added. He fumbled in the pouch at his belt and pulled out the gold ring he and Elenna had found in the Wildlands. "This belonged to the real Angelo," said Tom. "It was with his body in his tomb. Take it! If you spread the word, perhaps the people will rebel."

Harkman took the ring through the bars and stepped back. He stared at it for a moment, as if transfixed. Then he began to laugh.

"What's funny?" said Elenna, frowning.

"You two," said Captain Harkman. "How stupid you both are..."

Tom felt a shiver run down his spine. "Wait," he said. "Give it back!"

But it was too late.

Something strange was happening to Harkman. His armour was melting into vapour, floating away and disappearing. His face was changing too: his nose broadening, his hair growing long. In a moment, Harkman was gone, and King Angelo stood in his place, smoothing down his red cloak. He adjusted his crown and smiled.

Tom blinked. *It's not possible!*

"What are you?" whispered Elenna.

King Angelo just smiled wider.
"I could tell you, but why should
I bother? Tomorrow, I'm going to
execute all three of you!"

1

3

CUNNING

"He's some sort of shapeshifter," murmured Daltec, after King Angelo had walked away. His footsteps echoed on the stairs, then there was a heavy thump as the cell door closed.

Tom slammed a fist against the bars in frustration. *And now we've lost the ring too!* Without it, there was no way they could prove Angelo was a fraud.

Anger surged through Tom's body, and he grabbed hold of the bars, tugging as hard as he could. But the metal wouldn't budge.

"I've got another idea," said Elenna. She bent down and drew a metallic object from inside her boot.

Tom's heart leaped. "Is that an arrowhead?"

"I hid it there back in the Wildlands," Elenna explained. "Just in case Petra tried anything!"

Tom grinned at her. "Great thinking!"

Elenna jammed the arrowhead inside the lock. The metal scraped as she twisted it until – *click!*

Slowly, carefully, she pushed open the door. *Creeeeak!* The ancient hinges groaned, echoing through the dungeon. Elenna flinched. "Uh-oh," she murmured. "Better hurry!"

They all squeezed out into the corridor. A moment later, the door at the top of the stairs swung open. Swift Gareth came charging down the steps towards them, one hand on his sword hilt, ready to draw.

Daltec seized a flaming torch from the wall. His hands were still tied together, but he grasped it tightly.

"Take that!" roared the wizard, swinging the torch in a blazing arc. *CLONK!* The torch struck Gareth

hard on his helmet. Sparks flew, and
he staggered, then slumped to the
ground.

Elenna whistled. "Didn't think

you had it in you, Daltec."

"Come on," said Tom, once Elenna had sliced through the ropes round Daltec's wrists. "Before any of the other guards hear."

But as they set off, a low moan came from a cell nearby. Tom peered into the shadows and saw a figure curled up there. "It's Harkman!" he gasped. "The real one."

Elenna quickly picked the lock with her arrowhead, and Tom darted inside. The captain looked pale and thin, his face and arms covered with dark bruises and swellings. "It's good to see you," he grunted, as Tom lifted him up into a sitting position.

"You'd better wait here," said Tom.

"You can't fight in this state."

Harkman just chuckled. "Try and stop me. I've a bone to pick with that traitor king. I'm going to round up as many soldiers as I can – the ones who are loyal to Hugo."

"Good luck," said Tom. "Meanwhile, we'll find Angelo..."

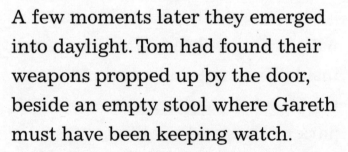

A few moments later they emerged into daylight. Tom had found their weapons propped up by the door, beside an empty stool where Gareth must have been keeping watch.

"Be careful," warned Daltec. The wizard was supporting Captain Harkman with one arm. "There are guards everywhere."

"Don't worry about us," said Elenna. "Just gather as many soldiers as you can."

Harkman nodded, and the pair set off, hobbling through the shadows by the palace wall.

Now to face the imposter...

Together Tom and Elenna crept towards the main palace building, crouching low so as not to be seen.

"I've never seen so many soldiers on patrol," whispered Elenna, casting a glance up at the walls.

Tom followed her gaze. He saw helmets glinting in the sunshine as Angelo's men marched up and down. "We can't go through the main gate," he said. "They'll see us for sure. But if we go through the palace kitchens..."

"...we can sneak up on Angelo!" finished Elenna.

Quickly, they darted through the courtyard to a side door. They sneaked through into a huge, cavern-like room full of steam, and the clatter of pots and pans. *The kitchens!* Cooks and maids turned to stare in astonishment, but Tom put a finger to his lips. *I just hope they're still loyal to King Hugo...*

Luckily, the servants just nodded back. Some even turned away, pretending they'd never seen him.

Tom and Elenna hurried through

the kitchens and up a winding
servants' staircase. "Let's try the
throne room," Tom whispered.

They turned into a narrow corridor
and pushed through a door. Tom
tensed, his eyes carefully tracking

round the room…

But there was no one there.

"It looks…different, don't you think?" said Elenna. She pointed at the tapestries that hung on the walls.

Tom peered closer. *Angelo's changed them all!* The old tapestries had shown brave deeds undertaken by old rulers of Avantia. But the new ones were decorated with Beasts. *And they're attacking humans!*

Tom recognised a three-headed dragon. *That's Torka!* Krotax was there too, and Querzol – all three of the Wildlands Beasts that Tom and Elenna had defeated. Villages were on fire, while people fled from the rampaging creatures.

"I don't like this," said Elenna, with a shiver. "It's like he's celebrating how the Beasts are tormenting people."

"Maybe he is," said a voice from behind.

Tom and Elenna spun round. A woman stepped out from behind a tapestry. She had unkempt grey hair, and wore a purple robe.

Tom gripped his sword tighter. *Kapra!*

"You know," said Petra's mother, "my daughter told me you were fools, but I really didn't think you'd be stupid enough to come back here."

Elenna charged. But she'd hardly taken two steps when Kapra flung out her arm. Purple light uncoiled from her fingertips and swept around Tom and Elenna. The light felt as solid as iron, and it pulled

them together like a lasso.

Tom and Elenna squirmed and fought against it, but their struggles only seemed to strengthen the bonds.

"I'm afraid I can't allow you children to ruin everything the way you usually do," said Kapra cheerfully.

"We saved your daughter's life," said Tom. "We're not your enemies!"

"Liar!" hissed Kapra. Her eyes flashed with hatred, and Tom felt his chest burning as the purple light closed in, tighter and tighter.

"I can't...breathe!" gasped Elenna.

Tom tried to draw air into his lungs, but it was no good. *She's going to choke us to death!*

LITTLE TADPOLE

"Mother! Stop!"

Tom raised his head at the cry.

Another figure had run into the room. *Petra!* Tom had never been so glad to see her in his life.

The purple light was suddenly gone, and the pressure vanished from Tom's chest. He fell forward, gasping. Elenna crouched beside him, coughing and spluttering just like Tom.

We're alive!

"My darling little tadpole," cooed Kapra, hobbling towards Petra. "Is

it really you?" She reached out with bony fingers, but Petra just folded her arms and turned up her nose.

"No thanks to you, Mother. Or have you forgotten how you abandoned me in a rat-infested cellar up on that mountainside?"

"Oh, don't be silly, tadpole," said Kapra. "Those were just harmless cockroaches! Besides, Xerkan told me that Torka would kill us both if I didn't do his bidding."

"Who's Xerkan?" asked Tom and Petra at the same time.

Kapra turned to glare at Tom. "Xerkan is the fourth Beast of the Wildlands, of course. The one who rules over the other three."

Tom frowned. "Tell me," he said, "is he some kind of shapeshifter?"

A nasty smile spread across Kapra's face. "Now he's beginning to understand..."

Tom felt a sick feeling swirling in his stomach. *We didn't abandon the Wildlands to the fourth Beast, after all. Xerkan has been in disguise in Avantia this whole time...*

"King Angelo is really Xerkan," whispered Elenna, her eyes wide with horror.

Kapra threw her hands up. "Finally! I can't believe the Avantians are too stupid to have figured it out. Even King Hugo was fooled, and he's supposed to be Angelo's brother! Idiots!" She cackled.

"Where is Xerkan now?" Tom asked.

Kapra shrugged. "In the royal bedchamber, probably. It's not easy keeping a different shape from your natural form, even for Xerkan. He has to rest for most of the day."

Shakily, Tom stood. He still felt weak from Kapra's spell, but he picked up his sword. "That's where we're going, then," he said firmly.

Kapra laughed. "That's where *you're* going. Petra and I are leaving this wretched kingdom at once."

She began to shuffle towards the door, but Petra stayed put. Tom saw that the young witch was frowning, as though she wasn't sure what to do.

"Tadpole?" said Kapra.

Petra shook her head. "I'm staying here."

"What?" exploded Kapra. "Let the Avantians deal with this!"

"Torka nearly killed me, Mother!" snapped Petra. "And you too. Don't you want to take revenge?"

"Think of your poor little tadpole," Elenna added.

Petra threw her a savage glare. But Kapra groaned and started walking towards her daughter. "Oh, very well. We'll pay back the Beast for his blackmail." She pointed a bony finger at Tom. "But I shall expect a nice fat reward from your king, boy!"

"If you help us, I'm sure you'll get what you deserve," said Tom. "Follow me, then."

The four of them crept through the palace. Tom's heart was pounding in his chest.

"What about the guards?" whispered Elenna, as they climbed the spiral steps towards the royal bedchamber. "I'm sure Xerkan will have soldiers outside the door."

"Don't you worry about them, my dear," said Kapra with a crooked smile. She twitched her fingers, and a soft blue light glowed around them all for an instant.

Tom frowned. "Was that a spell?

What did you do?"

He turned to Elenna and blinked.

She's vanished! Petra was gone too.

"Where are you, Tom?" came Elenna's anxious voice, from thin air.

"I've made you all invisible, you halfwits!" cackled Kapra, shaking her head at them. "Now follow me. Keep your mouths shut, and try not to bump into anything! Quickly now, the spell won't last for ever."

Tom tiptoed up the stairs behind Kapra. As they turned on to the landing, he saw a pair of soldiers on guard at the door to the royal bedchamber.

"Out of the way, imbeciles," said Kapra, with a wave of her hand. "I have news for the king!"

Tom saw the guards scowl, but they stood aside all the same. Kapra swept through the door, leaving it open so that Tom, Elenna and Petra could come after her. The door closed quietly behind them and the bolt slid across. *That must be Petra*, thought Tom. *Or maybe Elenna!*

"Greetings, Your Majesty," said Kapra.

A great four-poster bed stood in the middle of the stone floor, draped in red velvet curtains. Tom heard someone shift within, and the curtain stirred.

"What do you want, witch?" The voice that spoke was deep, with a strange accent. *Nothing like the fake Angelo's voice!*

Tom stepped forward, raising his

sword. "We want our true king back,"
he said.

There was a moment of silence,
then the fake king gave a low
chuckle. "An invisibility spell," he
scoffed. "How skilful of you, Kapra."

His laughter grew so loud that Tom
took a step back, grimacing at the
sound as it echoed through the room.
The curtain rippled like water as the
bed began to shake.

"What's happening?" gasped Tom.

"He's changing," said Kapra, her
eyes glinting. "Into his true form!"

TRUE FORM

Swwwwish! A curved silver claw sliced through the red curtain around the bed. *Crrrack!* The bed frame broke. Then a huge figure hauled itself free of the wreckage.

The fourth Beast of the Wildlands... Tom felt a cold shiver of fear at the sight of him.

Xerkan's skin was as grey as a

corpse's, and his head was huge, round and warty, with pointed ears. He glared at Tom with dull, purplish eyes, his thin lips pulling back to reveal jagged teeth every bit as sharp as the claws on each fingertip.

Elenna and Petra flickered suddenly into view, and Tom realised that Kapra's invisibility spell must have worn off.

The Beast can see us now!

Tom crouched down behind his shield, as Elenna whipped an arrow from her quiver and fitted it on her bowstring. Petra nervously edged behind her mother.

Xerkan lowered his head. "Traitor witch," he hissed, foul drool falling from his teeth to hit the floor with a *splat*. "You dare stand against me?"

Kapra swallowed hard. Then suddenly, she threw out both hands.

Fffzzzap! A bolt of purple light shot from her fingers. The Beast's hand was already raised like a shield. The magic struck his palm and shot straight back at Kapra. The old witch danced aside, and fragments of stone crumbled from the wall where the bolt hit.

Whhhssh! Elenna let fly with her arrow, which sank deep into the Beast's raised hand. Xerkan didn't even flinch. Instead, he just took the arrow between two fingers, plucked it out and threw it away. At once, his grey flesh closed over the wound.

Tom looked at Elenna, his own shock mirrored in her eyes. He knew they were thinking the same thing. *If Xerkan's wounds heal instantly, how can we possibly defeat him?*

The door shook as something thumped into it from outside. A soldier's voice roared, "Open up in the name of King Angelo!"

Xerkan's lips parted again in a savage grin. Then he lunged forward, swiping his claws like scythes.

Tom darted in front of Elenna. *THUMP!* He caught Xerkan's blow full on his shield. It swept him off his feet, and he hurtled across the room. He smacked into the wall, feeling

every bone in his body shuddering
as he slid to the floor.

He gritted his teeth, fighting to
ignore the pain. *We need to distract
the Beast...play for time...* He
glanced round the room, his eyes

falling on a tapestry hanging on the far wall. *That might work!*

Elenna fired another arrow, but Xerkan knocked the shaft out of the air with a flick of a claw.

Quickly, Tom darted behind the Beast, snatched a corner of the tapestry and tore it down. "Elenna!" he called.

Xerkan was prowling towards Kapra and Petra now, who were both cowering behind a carved wooden chest in the corner. Two strings of drool dangled from his teeth, trickling down his chest.

Elenna dashed to Tom's side and grabbed hold of another corner of the tapestry.

"Now!" shouted Tom.

Together they rushed across the room, dragging the wall hanging. Then they hurled it over the Beast.

Xerkan let out a howl of fury and slashed at the tapestry as it completely covered his head.

"Hold him down!" Tom shouted.

Kapra and Petra ran out from behind the chest, grabbing a corner each, along with Tom and Elenna. Together they dragged the tapestry to the ground, with the Beast trapped under it.

The Beast writhed beneath the heavy material, and it was all Tom could do to hang on to his corner. "Give up, Xerkan!" he yelled.

At once, the Beast went still. Tom could hardly believe it. *Is he really going to surrender?*

Then King Angelo's voice could be heard. "Please..." he begged. "Is it gold you want? You shall have it, if you'll only spare my life."

Elenna frowned. "What's he playing at?"

Before Tom could reply, there was a hefty *THUMP* against the door. "Open up, or we'll break through!" shouted a soldier.

At once, Tom understood the Beast's scheme. His heart plummeted. "Xerkan must have changed back into Angelo," he said. "Any minute now, the guards will break through. They'll think we're trying to kill the king!"

From beneath the tapestry, the fake King Angelo let out a low chuckle. "You can't win…"

THUMP! Another blow shook the door, and the hinges cracked.

We've only got a few moments…

"The window," Tom said, pointing. "It's the only way out of here."

Petra made a face. "Have you gone mad? We're at the top of a tower! We'll be smashed to bits on the courtyard below."

"Oh, don't be such a baby," said Kapra, rolling her eyes. "My magic will keep us safe."

CRASH! The door slammed open.

Two soldiers stumbled in, holding a small battering ram between them.

At once Kapra and Petra let go of the tapestry, ran to the window and threw themselves out of it. More soldiers rushed into the chamber, each carrying a loaded crossbow.

"Wait – this isn't the real king..." Tom began, raising his hands.

But Angelo struggled free of the heavy material, pushing his crown back on to his head. "They attacked me!" he gasped. "Don't let them get away!" He glared at Tom. But for an instant his lips twisted into a smile, and his eyes went dull purple again.

"Run!" yelled Elenna. She darted

to the window, and dived through it. Five crossbow bolts shot through the air. *Whsssh!* Tom ducked, hearing the bolts clatter against the stone walls.

As the soldiers began to reload, Tom ran for the window too, hopped up on the sill and flung himself out into nothingness.

For an instant his body seemed to hang there. Then he began to drop, face first. He could see the paving stones of the courtyard far below, but getting closer, faster and faster... The wind buffeted his face and flung back his hair. His heart thundered in his chest.

If only I still had the magic of Arcta's feather to slow my fall...

He closed his eyes.

Then he felt something press against his whole body. Something soft and pillowy, as though he had fallen into the gentle palm of a giant.

Tom opened his eyes. He was lying on a purple cloud, drifting slowly downwards. He turned his head and saw Elenna floating on a cloud of her own.

Kapra's magic!

Relief flooded Tom's body as the cloud touched down in the courtyard and billowed away in puffs of purple smoke. He landed next to Elenna, with a soft bump, on the stone below. *Not a scratch between us!*

"A little 'thank you' would be nice," said Kapra. Tom turned to see the witch and her daughter nearby. "After all, I did save your life."

"Yes," said Elenna, "for now." She pointed to a corner of the courtyard.

Soldiers were spilling out of a door there, dozens of them, armour clanking as they ran straight towards Tom and Elenna. They had crossbows, spears and shields. *Too many to fight*, thought Tom, as the soldiers surrounded them.

He glanced up at the tower they had fallen from. Angelo was leaning out of the window, silhouetted against the bright blue sky.

"Kill the intruders!" he roared. "Kill them now!"

The soldiers lifted their crossbows, taking aim at Tom and Elenna.

This is it, thought Tom. *This is where my Quest ends...* "Long live King Hugo!" he cried.

KAPRA'S REVENGE

A loud, slow creak of wood sounded across the courtyard.

"The gates!" shouted a soldier.

Tom and Elenna turned. The gates of the Palace were slowly swinging open. Tom's heart leaped as he spotted Captain Harkman to one side, heaving at the winch.

"The true king is here!" he yelled.

"All kneel for the true king!"

Elenna frowned. "Surely he can't mean..."

Horses swept in through the open gates. And when Tom saw the riders, he could hardly believe his eyes.

King Hugo and Queen Aroha rode in the lead, their armour glinting in the sunshine. Behind them rode two columns of armoured soldiers carrying lances. They were all women, and their white horsehair crests streamed as they galloped into the courtyard.

"It's the Warrior Women of Tangala!" gasped Elenna.

Tom grinned. "Daltec's message must have made it through after all!"

"Form up!" yelled one of Angelo's soldiers. At once the circle around Tom and Elenna broke apart and re-formed into a ragged line, with crossbows, spears and swords all pointed at the Tangalans. Queen Aroha held up a hand, and the Warrior Women reined in their horses. They were a stone's throw from King Angelo's soldiers.

Tom's stomach squirmed with worry. *If just one of those soldiers fires, it will cause a full-scale battle!* He noticed that Kapra and Petra had taken shelter behind a pile of barrels.

"There'll be no blood spilt here," said King Hugo. His voice echoed through the courtyard. "Let me speak with my brother!"

Tom glanced up, and saw that Angelo had disappeared.

A moment later, a door swung open at the bottom of the tower, and Angelo came striding out. He wore a puzzled smile. "Brother!" said Angelo, holding out his hands. "It's good to see your face. But why have you brought soldiers to my palace? Have you forgotten that I'm the rightful king?"

King Hugo looked lost for words. He blushed deeply and shook his head. "Forgive me, I..."

"It's a trick!" yelled Elenna. "He's an imposter, Your Highness!"

"He's a Beast," added Tom. "He's Xerkan of the Wildlands, and he can change his shape whenever he wants!"

King Angelo just chuckled. "Poor Tom and Elenna," he said. "I'm afraid they've spent so long battling monsters, they now can't help seeing them everywhere they look! And of course it's a shock to have a new king." He turned back to Hugo, and smiled. "Perhaps I was harsh to send you away, brother. The wars of the north have made me less than patient. Will you stay? Will you help me become the ruler Avantians deserve?"

Hugo nodded slowly. Even Queen

Aroha smiled at Angelo.

They're falling for it! Tom was about to rush forward, when a figure darted from the shadows. It was Kapra. Tom saw a glint of steel in her hand. *A knife...* Then the witch plunged it deep into King Angelo's back.

"Nobody blackmails Kapra!" she screamed.

A great gasp went up from both the Tangalans and the Avantians.

Angelo staggered. His mouth fell open, and his face turned pale. Then he began to shudder. In moments his whole body was shaking.

Angelo's crown and robe began to melt, turning into coloured smoke that drifted away to the sky. He hunched over, his body growing, his fingers stretching into silver claws. At the same time, his skin turned ashen grey, his hair vanished and his head began to bulge grotesquely.

Everyone watched, silent with horror, as the creature raised his head and glared around with purple eyes.

Xerkan backed away, like a cornered animal. He reached behind him with one long arm, tugged the blade free and tossed it aside. Oily black blood spattered on the paving stones.

"Filthy witch!" he snarled, baring his sharp teeth.

Before Kapra could react, Xerkan snatched hold of her by the ankle. He dragged her off her feet, whirled her around his head and threw her.

Tom winced as the witch came crashing down on the ground. *Thump!*

"Mother!" cried Petra. She ran over and kneeled beside Kapra's body.

"What are you waiting for?" shrieked Xerkan. He aimed a curved claw at the Tangalans. "Attack!"

His soldiers hesitated, glancing uncertainly at their master.

"You fools!" snarled Xerkan. "Betray me now, and you will all be thrown back in the gaol. Fight for me, and you shall have a pardon and a heap of gold!"

"You can't trust him!" shouted Tom.

But already the soldiers were raising their weapons and forming a line. Then they marched towards the waiting Tangalans, their boots thumping in time as they went into battle.

"Kill them all!" roared Xerkan.

7

HUNTING GROUND

"Capture the Beast!" cried Queen Aroha.

The Tangalan warriors spurred on their horses. Hoofbeats echoed through the courtyard, as the Warrior Women galloped at their opponents. *CRASH!* They met the Avantians like a wave breaking on a rock.

The air filled with the clash of steel, screams and war cries. Horses reared. Soldiers scurried to and fro, jabbing with their swords while the Tangalans thrust their lances. Tom spotted Harkman in the fray, the captain slashing at Xerkan's soldiers with a double-headed axe.

Tom was just about to rush in himself, when he felt Elenna's hand on his sword arm. "Xerkan's escaped!" she hissed.

Sure enough, Tom couldn't see any sign of the Beast. Then he spotted something. A monstrous shadow, flitting past the palace gates...

We've got to get after him!

Tom and Elenna ducked and dodged through the battle, skirting around the side of the courtyard. Tom cast one last glance back, and saw King Hugo and Queen Aroha fighting bravely on horseback, swords flashing. *Good luck, Your Majesties...* Then he and Elenna slipped out into the City.

The streets were deserted. But Tom saw citizens here and there, peering through windows or from behind doors. *They look even more scared than they were before!*

"There," said Elenna suddenly, pointing to one side. Tom saw a shadow flicker past the end of an alley. He plunged in, following as fast as he could. When he came out on the other side he paused, panting. He stood in a narrow street which ran both ways, but Xerkan was nowhere to be seen.

Nothing moved. The noise of the battle was just a distant thunder, and Tom felt a cold prickle of fear run down his spine.

Where are you, Xerkan?

A low chuckle sounded, and Tom spun round. Still nothing. He crept down the street, with Elenna close behind. At the end there was a little square, with a dried-up old fountain and empty houses all around.

"I can see you," came a sudden

hiss from Xerkan.

Tom's heart lurched. He looked around, gripping his sword tight. But he couldn't tell where the voice had come from.

Xerkan laughed again. "This city is a fine hunting ground, Tom," he whispered. The voice seemed to come from nowhere and everywhere at once. "So much more interesting than the Wildlands. So many places to hide..."

A claw scraped on stone.

"Come out, coward!" cried Elenna.

"If you insist," said Xerkan. "I will enjoy killing you, Elenna. You too, Master of the Beasts. When I've stolen your shape, I shall lure the

Good Beasts to me, one by one. And one by one, they'll die. Avantia will be left utterly defenceless!"

Xerkan let out another cackle.

There! Tom spotted another flash of movement. It was a shadow, flickering on the ground beside an ancient, round stone tower that rose up over the corner of the square. He caught Elenna's eyes, and saw that she'd seen it too. Silently, he pointed, and Elenna nodded. Then they set out, each creeping around one side of the tower.

Tom gripped his sword and shield even tighter as he tiptoed, following the curve of the wall. He licked his lips. Xerkan was surely hiding there, behind the tower. *Any moment now...*

A shape came from the shadows. Tom raised his sword. Then he froze.

"Elenna!" he whispered.

She lowered her bow and arrow. "The Beast isn't here," she muttered. "Where—"

Dust and stones sprinkled down on to them. Tom glanced up, and his stomach lurched with shock.

Xerkan!

The Beast was crouching above them like a gigantic spider. He was halfway up the old tower, clinging to the stones with his claws. His eyes gleamed down at them. Then, with a rending sound, he tore a chunk of rock from the tower.

"Take cover!" Elenna yelled.

Tom and Elenna flung themselves
over a low wall and ducked down
behind it as the rock exploded right
where they'd been standing. Peering

cautiously over the wall, Tom saw
Xerkan rip another chunk of rock
from the tower. He flung it, and Tom
dodged just in time.

Thunk! The rock hit the wall.

"If he carries on, he'll pull the
whole tower down!" hissed Elenna.

Tom's heart was racing, but he
knew they couldn't hide for ever.
"We've got to face him," he said. "If
he gets away, there's no knowing
what damage he could cause."

But when he looked at the tower,
Xerkan had gone.

"I don't understand," said Elenna,
rising beside Tom.

Footsteps sounded from an alley.
Tom turned, crouching behind his

shield. But when the figure turned the corner, he relaxed and smiled.

"King Hugo!" he said.

The king was panting and sweating, his sword dangling from one hand. "The battle is almost won," he gasped. "Where is Xerkan?"

Tom opened his mouth to reply. Then a shout came from the square.

"Get away from him, Tom! It's a trick!"

Spinning round, Tom froze with shock. Standing there was another man, wearing the same clothes, carrying the same sword...and with the same face!

Tom glanced at Elenna. "Which is the real king?"

THE RIGHTFUL KING

Tom raised his sword. He wanted nothing more than to charge in and fight the Beast... *But there's no way of knowing which of my opponents is really Xerkan!*

The first Hugo stepped into the square, bringing his sword up into a fighting position.

The second Hugo backed away
behind the fountain and crouched
low, his gaze locked on his
opponent. "I'm the real king, Tom,"
he called.

"He's lying," said the first Hugo.

"I'm the real king!"

Tom heard the creak of a bowstring, and saw Elenna taking aim with an arrow. "Which one do I shoot?" she muttered.

Tom shook his head. "I've no idea!"

The first Hugo sprang at his opponent, sword flashing through the air. *Clang!* The blade glanced off the stone fountain.

The second Hugo had ducked away, but now he came darting in, thrusting his sword in a lunge. There was a scrape of metal as his opponent parried. Then the blades met as the kings struck at each other, over and over.

The clatter of metal echoed

through the square, and dust drifted up from the two kings' shuffling boots. Tom winced at the sheer strength of each blow. Very soon, both men were panting and sweating. Their blades clashed again, and they shoved, stumbling apart for a moment.

Elenna shook her head in frustration. "I can't believe I'm saying this...but I wish Petra was here! We need magic to tell these two apart."

The second Hugo darted forward to attack. But his boot slipped, and he skidded on one knee.

Quick as lightning, the first Hugo kicked the sword from his opponent's hand. It spun, glinting, through the air and skittered to the ground, far out of reach. The second Hugo tried to get to his feet, but the first Hugo pushed him down and held the edge of his blade against his neck.

Tom rushed forward. "It's over!" he said. "The fight ends here."

The first Hugo stared at Tom in surprise. Then, slowly, he shook his head. "Don't be foolish, Tom," he said. "This isn't over while one of us still breathes."

He stepped back and lifted his great sword, two-handed, ready to strike the kneeling king's head from his body.

"No!" yelled Elenna.

And in that moment, Tom knew what he had to do. He stepped forward and caught the blow full on his shield. *Thump!* His arm juddered with pain.

The first Hugo's smile twisted into a savage scowl. He raised his sword again. But before he could strike, Tom drove his own sword hard into the king's chest.

Tom heard Elenna gasp in shock. The first Hugo's mouth gaped open wide. He stared at the blade embedded in his chest. "What have you done?" he croaked.

Tom's heart was hammering, but he knew he had made the right decision.

"You're Xerkan," he said. "The real King Hugo would never kill someone in cold blood. Not even a Beast of the Wildlands."

The first Hugo staggered back, with Tom's sword still buried deep within him. Blood spattered on the paving stones. He groaned. Then the groan changed. It became a chuckle. Then a laugh, loud and triumphant.

The fake Hugo's armour turned to smoke, spiralling away into the air. His back arched, and his head bulged, and in moments the true form of Xerkan was revealed. The ghoulish creature stretched up to his full height, casting a shadow across the square. He tugged Tom's sword from his wound and tossed it to the ground with a clatter.

"How clever you are, Master of the Beasts," hissed Xerkan. "Such a shame that it won't save you. No weapon can harm me. You have only delayed your own death!"

Xerkan prowled towards Tom, Hugo and Elenna. His grey claws gleamed.

Tom curled his fingers into a fist. *I've got no sword, but at least I'll die fighting!*

Xerkan's head jerked to one side as a trumpet blast rang out, his purple eyes widening as someone came galloping into the square on a white horse. *Queen Aroha!* She crouched low over the saddle, charging straight at Xerkan.

"She'll crash right into him!" gasped Elenna.

But at the last moment, Aroha tugged on the reins. Her horse reared, driving its front hooves into Xerkan's gut.

The Beast howled, doubled up and

staggered. His foot slipped on Tom's sword, and he tumbled backwards. His back thumped into the half-ruined old tower at the edge of the square. Then Tom heard a low rumbling, and a cracking of rock.

Xerkan glanced upwards, and for an instant Tom saw sheer terror in his strange purplish eyes. His lips parted in shock.

With a deafening crash, the tower came crumbling down. A thundering avalanche of ancient stones rained on the Beast, jolting and bouncing through the square. The ground shook and a great cloud of dust rose up. Tom ducked down, closed his eyes and covered his mouth with his sleeve.

At last, as the sound of the falling tower died away, Tom heard new sounds filling the square: the clatter of horseshoes, the clinking of armour and the shouts of soldiers.

Blinking, he made out shapes through the rising dust. Tangalan warriors on horseback were there, one carrying a trumpet. There were Avantian soldiers too, and Captain Harkman, wielding his battle-axe. They all stared in amazement at the ruins of the tower.

As the dust cleared, Tom saw that half the square was heaped with broken stone. Among the rubble, nothing could be seen of Xerkan but one grey hand poking free.

Tom watched the pale claws twitching, trying to grip hold of something. They scrabbled, hopelessly, seeming weaker with every movement. Then the fingers flopped.

It's over. The final Beast of the Wildlands is defeated!

Tom heard a scrape of stirrups, and saw Queen Aroha swing herself from her horse. She dashed across the square to King Hugo, pulled him to his feet and flung her arms around him.

"Long live Queen Aroha!" shouted Captain Harkman. "Long live King Hugo!"

As the Tangalans and Avantians took up the cry, Tom felt his heart lift with relief. He could hardly believe it. *The Quest is over. At last!*

Two more figures came hobbling into the square, and Tom grinned. Petra was supporting her mother, who looked dazed but unharmed.

"What's going on here?" said the young witch. "Don't tell me we missed out on all the danger?"

"Typical," grunted Elenna. But Tom saw that she was grinning.

"Is Aduro back yet?" asked Tom.

It was three days after the battle in the City, and he and Elenna were following Daltec through the corridors of the palace. His body still ached from the fight with Xerkan, but a good feast and an even better night's sleep had made him feel a hundred times stronger.

Daltec smiled. "He returned this morning. With Prince Thomas, of course. And now the kingdom is safe once more!"

They reached the throne room, and Tom breathed a sigh of relief. Xerkan's horrible tapestries had been taken down, and soldiers were on ladders, hanging up the banners of Avantia in their place. King Hugo stood below, directing them carefully, while Queen Aroha cradled baby

Prince Thomas in her arms.

"Your Majesties! Master of the Beasts!"

Tom smiled to see Captain Harkman approaching. His old friend was still a little pale and thin from his time in the dungeon, but the sparkle was back in his eye. He kneeled before the king.

"My men have cleared the rubble," said Harkman. "They found no sign of Xerkan's body. But they did find something else."

The captain held out a hand, and Tom saw something gleaming in his palm. It was the gold ring which had once belonged to the real Prince Angelo. *The one Xerkan stole from us in the dungeon.*

King Hugo reached for it, then hesitated. Tom's heart almost broke to see the look on the king's face. Grief was written deep in his eyes.

To think your brother was alive, then find out it was all a lie... It must feel like losing him all over again.

For a moment the throne room was silent. Then a familiar voice spoke from the doorway. "It is yours, Your Majesty." The old wizard Aduro shuffled in, smiling kindly. "It once belonged to your father, and his father before him. It shall always belong to the rightful king of Avantia."

King Hugo nodded. Then a sad

smile spread across his face, and he took the ring and slipped it on to his finger. "One day it will belong to Prince Thomas," he said.

The little baby gurgled in Queen Aroha's arms, and chuckles sounded

through the throne room. Tom felt
as though all the sorrow had melted
away at once.

King Hugo turned to Tom and
Elenna. "On behalf of Avantia, we
thank you," he said. "If you had
not journeyed to the Wildlands,
Xerkan's lies would never have been
uncovered, and the Beast would have
destroyed the kingdom."

"Your bravery is astonishing,"
added Queen Aroha. "To take on
such a dangerous Quest, and with no
magical powers..."

Aduro shook his head. "Forgive me,
Your Majesty. But it's not the Golden
Armour or magical jewels that make
a Master of the Beasts. When Tom

first came to the City, a simple farm boy from Errinel, he had nothing but his wits. But he had then what he has now...great courage in his heart. That is all a hero truly needs."

"Not all," said Tom. "He also needs a good friend at his side. One who'll face any danger with him."

He smiled at Elenna, and she smiled back at him.

As cheers rose up all around, Tom felt his heart filling with joy.

Whatever peril threatens Avantia, Elenna and I will always be ready to face it!

THE END

CONGRATULATIONS, YOU HAVE COMPLETED THIS QUEST!

At the end of each chapter you were awarded a special gold coin. The QUEST in this book was worth an amazing 8 coins.

Look at the Beast Quest totem picture opposite to see how far you've come in your journey to become

MASTER OF THE BEASTS.

The more books you read, the more coins you will collect!

Do you want your own
Beast Quest Totem?

1. Cut out and collect the coin below
2. Go to the Beast Quest website
3. Download and print out your totem
4. Add your coin to the totem

www.beastquest.co.uk

8

REA█ THE B███KS, ████LLECT THE ████INS!

EARN COINS FOR EVERY CHAPTER YOU READ!

550+ COINS
MASTER OF THE BEASTS

410 COINS
HERO

350 COINS
WARRIOR

230 COINS
KNIGHT

180 COINS
SQUIRE

44 COINS
PAGE

8 COINS
APPRENTICE

550+
515
480
445
410
395
380
365
350
320
290
260
230
212
206
191
180
158
132
78
44
30
15
8

BeastQuest
NEW BLOOD
ADAM BLADE

Meet three new heroes with the power to tame the Beasts!

Amy, Charlie and Sam – three children from our world – are about to discover the powerful legacy that binds them together.

They are descendants of the *Guardians of Avantia,* an elite group of heroes trained by Tom himself.

Now the time has come for a new generation to unlock the power of the Beasts and fulfil their destiny.

Read on for a sneak peek at how the Guardians first left Avantia by magic...

Karita of Banquise gazed in awe at Tom, Avantia's mighty, bearded Master of the Beasts.

Under his leadership, she and her companions would today face their greatest challenge.

Tom pointed towards the brooding Gorgonian castle. "We must recover the chest of Beast Eggs Malvel stole," he reminded them. His fierce blue eyes moved from Karita to the others. Dell of Stonewin, whose bloodline connected him to Beasts of Fire; Fern of Errinel, linked to Storm Beasts; Gustus of Colton, bonded with Water Beasts.

"Malvel will be expecting an attack," Tom said. "His power is lessened, but he is still formidable." His eyes locked on Karita. "Stealth will be our greatest ally."

Karita felt as though her whole life had been a preparation for this moment. Countless hours spent studying the ancient tomes, day after day of gruelling combat training, months learning how to influence the will of Stealth Beasts and control the powers that filled the Arcane Band at her wrist.

But was she ready?

She gazed into Tom's face, and her doubts faded.

Yes!

A low rumble came from the

castle. Flashes of green lightning shot from the clouds as a swarm of screeching creatures erupted from the battlements.

Karita shuddered as Malvel's hideous minions streaked through the sky. They were man-sized, with white hides, limbs tipped with hooked claws and gaping jaws lined with sharp teeth. Their leathery wings cracked like whips.

"Karrakhs!" muttered Tom. "Karita – go!"

She nodded and slipped away behind jagged rocks. She turned to see the swarm of foul creatures engulf her companions. Tom's sword flashed. Howls rang out from the Karrakhs. The Guardians were using

Beast Quest

OUT NOW!

The epic adventure is brought to life on **Xbox One** and **PS4** for the first time ever!

Karita saw the walls of the portal writhing and distorting. Malvel's fireballs were making it unstable. At any moment it might vanish!

Tom was knocked back by a torrent of green fire as the wizard turned and leaped into the portal. Karita flung herself after him.

"No! Karita!" The last thing she heard was Tom's voice. "The portal is in flux! You could be sent anywhere!"

And then there was nothing but a rushing wind and howling darkness, as she plunged into the unknown.

Look out for
Beast Quest: New Blood
to find out what happens next!

Tom. "Stop him!"

Gustus ran at the wizard and wrested the chest from his grip. Roaring in anger, Malvel launched a fireball, but Fern managed to shove Gustus out of its path. But the force of her push knocked Gustus into the portal. With a stifled cry, he and the chest of eggs were gone.

"No!" Fern shouted, diving in after him. With a shout, Dell ran after her.

"Wait!" shouted Tom.

"It's our duty to protect the eggs!" Dell called back as he disappeared into the swirling portal.

Malvel sprang forward, but Tom bounded in front of him, holding him back with his spinning blade as the wizard hurled magical fireballs.

burning green. Before he could strike, the door burst open and Tom and the Guardians rushed into the room.

"No!" roared Malvel. "Where are my Karrakhs?"

"Defeated!" shouted Tom, whirling his sword to deflect Malvel's green flames. "Guardians! Take the eggs!"

Fern dived for the chest, but a blast from the wizard knocked her over.

"The eggs are mine!" howled Malvel. He traced a large circle of fire in the air. There was a blast of hot wind as the flaming hoop crackled and spat.

Malvel snatched up the chest and turned to the heart of the fiery circle.

"He's opened a portal!" shouted

can hatch a Beast Egg."

Karita swallowed hard, seeking a way to escape.

"You and your friends will hatch these Beasts and I will drink in their power," growled the wizard. "I will become mighty again and Avantia will bow before me!"

"I'm not afraid of you!" Karita shouted.

A ball of green fire exploded from Malvel's hand. Karita dived aside, seared by the heat.

She leaped up, thrusting her right arm towards the wizard. The Arcane Band began to form a weapon, but another blast of fire sent her sliding across the floor.

Malvel loomed over her, both hands

She came to a circular room, and saw the chest standing by the wall. Her heart hammering, Karita opened the lid and gazed down at the eggs. They were different sizes, shapes and colours. One slipped from the pile and she caught it in her gloved hand. It was pale blue, about the size of a goose egg. Acting on instinct, she slipped it inside her breastplate.

Crash!

She spun around. Malvel stood against the room's closed door.

"Did you really think you could enter my domain unseen?" he snarled, a green glow igniting in his palm. His voice was weaker than she'd imagined. "I *wanted* you to come here. After all, only a Guardian their Arcane Bands to form weapons that spun and slashed!

Karita raced for the castle, keeping low behind the ridge of rocks. Reaching the walls, she climbed up a gnarled vine and found a narrow window to crawl through. She looked back again. Tom and the Guardians had battled their way through the castle gates.

Well fought!

She dropped into a room and crept to the door. Torches burned in the corridor, casting shadows. The castle was silent, but Karita felt a growing dread as she slipped along the walls.

She knew where the chest of Beast eggs was hidden. But would Malvel allow her to get to them?